MADDIE AND MABEL
KNOW THEY CAN

To Chris, for always knowing I could. −K.A.

To Nora and Louisa, my favorite pair of sisters −T.M.

Maddie and Mabel Know They Can is published by
Kind World Publishing, PO Box 22356, Eagan, MN 55122
www.kindworldpublishing.com

Text copyright © 2023 by Kari Allen
Illustrations copyright © 2023 by Tatjana Mai-Wyss
Cover design by Tim Palin Creative

Published in 2023 by Kind World Publishing.

Printed in China.

ISBN 978-1-63894-019-7 (hardcover)

Library of Congress Control Number: 2022945086

MADDIE AND MABEL
KNOW THEY CAN

By Kari Allen
Illustrated by Tatjana Mai-Wyss

Kind WOrld
PUBLISHING

Eagan, Minnesota

CHAPTERS

Sisters 6

Flowers 14

For Sale 30

The Fall 52

The Ride 68

SISTERS

Maddie and Mabel are sisters.

Maddie is the big sister.

Mabel is the little sister.

Mabel has a lot of ideas.

Maddie likes to try new things.

Sometimes Maddie solves problems.

Sometimes Mabel does.

Mabel and Maddie are sisters and friends
and problem solvers too.

THE FLOWERS

Mabel was outside.

Maddie was not.

"Maddie!" Mabel shouted. "Something terrible has happened."

"Oh no!" said Maddie. "What is wrong?"

"My flowers are gone. They were here yesterday," said Mabel.

Mabel sniffled sadly. She asked, "Maddie, where did my flowers go?"

Maddie wanted to help.
She looked around the yard.

"Are these your flowers?" Maddie asked.

"No," said Mabel. "My flowers are not blue."

"Are these your flowers?" asked Maddie.

"No," said Mabel. "My flowers are
not orange."

"What color are your flowers?"
asked Maddie.

"My flowers are happy flowers," said Mabel.
"They are yellow flowers."

"Yellow flowers?" Maddie asked.

"Yes," Mabel said.

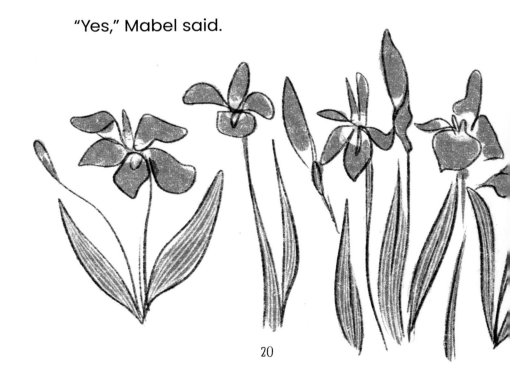

"We do not have yellow flowers in
our garden," Maddie said.

"They were not in our garden," said
Mabel. "They were in our yard.
All over the yard."

"The dandelions?" asked Maddie.

"Yes," said Mabel. "They are my favorite."

"Dandelions don't last as long as other flowers. They change," said Maddie.

Mabel did not know what to say.

But Maddie knew what to do.

"Here," she said. "Make a wish and blow."

"What do we do now?" asked Mabel.

"Now," said Maddie, "we wait."

"For how long?" asked Mabel.

"Until it is time," said Maddie.

FOR SALE

One morning Mabel woke up early.

An idea woke her up.

Mabel was small,
but she had a big, loud idea.

Mabel put a table at the end
of the driveway.

She made a sign.

She drew a cup.

"What if we . . . " asked Maddie.

Mabel shook her head. "This is my idea," she said.

Mabel sat.

Mabel waited.

Maddie watched.

No one came.

It was hot.

Mabel called out,
"Lemonade for sale!"
No one came.

Mabel and Maddie looked
up and down the road.
No customers.

"What about . . . " said Maddie.

"Nope!" said Mabel.
"This time it is my idea."

Mabel tried counting cars,
but there were no cars to count.

Mabel stacked her cups into a tower.

Mabel made a bigger sign.
There was no one to see it.

"I give up," Mabel said.

Mabel unstacked her cups.

She folded her sign.

"One cup of lemonade, please," said a voice.
It was Maddie.

Mabel filled a cup up to the top.
She handed it to Maddie.

"Thank you," said Mabel. "For your help."
Maddie smiled.

Maddie counted her coins.

"How much?" she asked.

"For my first customer?" said Mabel.

"I'm your only customer," said Maddie.

"Free!" said Mabel.

THE FALL

Maddie was learning something new.
Sometimes new things can be hard.

"This is impossible," said Maddie.
"I keep falling over."

"Have you tried going fast?"
asked Mabel.

"I tried going fast," said Maddie.

"Did it work?" asked Mabel.

"No," said Maddie. "Fast was
not the answer."

"What else have you tried?" asked Mabel.

"I tried going slow," said Maddie.

"Did going slow work?" asked Mabel.

"No," said Maddie. "Going slow did
not work at all."

"I haven't tried *not* trying," said Maddie.
"I haven't tried giving up."

"You could try giving up," said Mabel.

Maddie and Mabel thought about this.
While they thought, it started to rain.

It rained and rained.
The ground was wet.
Maddie was wet.
But Mabel was not.

Mabel sat under their tree.
She patted the spot next to her.

"I can't do it," said Maddie.
Mabel waited.

"Maybe not," said Mabel.

"I don't think that is the answer I want,"
said Maddie.

"No," said Mabel. "Maybe not."

It was still
raining.

"I can't try in the rain," said Maddie.

"No," said Mabel. "You can't."

"I will have to wait," said Maddie.

"I will wait with you," said Mabel.

Mabel and Maddie
listened to the rain
and leaned on their tree
and waited.

THE RIDE

Maddie was ready.
Maddie was ready
with a plan
and her bike
and hope.

Mabel was ready.
Mabel was ready
with signs
and cheers
and love.

Maddie took a deep breath.

Mabel took a deep breath.

"Ow," Maddie said.

"I thought you would do it," said Mabel.

"Me too," said Maddie. "But I didn't."

"No, you didn't," said Mabel. "Not yet."

Maddie and Mabel flopped down.

"Look," said Maddie.
"Your flowers are back."

Mabel nodded.

"We had to wait," said Maddie.

"We did," said Mabel.

"Sometimes we have to wait until it's time,"
said Maddie.

That's true," said Mabel. "What do we do
while we wait?"

Maddie looked at the flowers.
She looked at her sister.

"We try again," said Maddie.

And that's what they did.

MAKE A KINDER WORLD

In these stories, Maddie and Mabel help each other out. How do you help others?

TALK ABOUT IT

Have you ever been disappointed? How did you feel? What did you do to change that feeling or find a different way of looking at the problem?

Have you ever had an idea that someone else thought was their idea too?

How did you move forward with that idea?

Do you get nervous when you try something new? What helps you get calm?

Maddie and Mabel talk about waiting. Why is waiting sometimes an important step?

CONNECT TO YOUR STORY

Write or draw about a time you had to try again.

How did it feel to start over? Did it work the first time? What was hard about trying again?